AR: L-6.4/ P-1.0

W9-DDL-184

CONTINENTS OF THE WORLD

DISCOVERING
AFRICA'S
LAND, PEOPLE, AND WILDLIFE

A MyReportLinks.com Book

Aileen Weintraub

MyReportLinks.com Books

an imprint of

Enslow Publishers, Inc.

Box 398, 40 Industrial Road
Berkeley Heights, NJ 07922
USA

MyReportLinks.com Books, an imprint of Enslow Publishers, Inc. MyReportLinks®
is a registered trademark of Enslow Publishers, Inc.

Copyright © 2004 by Enslow Publishers, Inc.

All rights reserved.

No part of this book may be reproduced by any means
without the written permission of the publisher.

Library of Congress Cataloging-in-Publication Data

Weintraub, Aileen, 1973–
  Discovering Africa's land, people, and wildlife / Aileen Weintraub.
     v. cm. — (Continents of the world)
Includes bibliographical references and index.
Contents: Overview of the continent — Land and climate — Plant and
animal life — People and culture — Economy — Exploration and history.

 ISBN-10: 0-7660-5204-4
 1. Africa—Juvenile literature. [1. Africa.] I. Title. II. Series.
 DT3.W37 2004
 916—dc22

                                   2003014486

 ISBN-13: 978-0-7660-5204-8

Printed in the United States of America

10 9 8 7 6 5 4 3 2

To Our Readers:
Through the purchase of this book, you and your library gain access to the Report Links that specifically back up this book.
The Publisher will provide access to the Report Links that back up this book and will keep these Report Links up to date on **www.myreportlinks.com** for five years from the book's first publication date.
We have done our best to make sure all Internet addresses in this book were active and appropriate when we went to press. However, the author and the Publisher have no control over, and assume no liability for, the material available on those Internet sites or on other Web sites they may link to.
The usage of the MyReportLinks.com Books Web site is subject to the terms and conditions stated on the Usage Policy Statement on **www.myreportlinks.com**.
A password may be required to access the Report Links that back up this book. The password is found on the bottom of page 4 of this book.
Any comments or suggestions can be sent by e-mail to comments@myreportlinks.com or to the address on the back cover.

Photo Credits: ArtToday.com, p. 35; Artville, p. 1; Clipart.com, p. 40; © 2000, University of Wisconsin System Board of Regents, p. 19; © BBC MM II, p. 42; © Copyright The British Museum, p. 12; © Corel Corporation, pp. 10, 14, 21, 22, 26, 28, 29, 33, 37, 44; CultureFocus.com, p. 24; Enslow Publishers, Inc., p. 17; MyReportLinks.com Books, p. 4; National Museum of African Art/Smithsonian Institution, p. 31; Photos.com, p. 3; South African National Parks, p. 38.

Cover Photo: Artville; Clipart.com; © Corel Corporation; Photos.com.

Contents

MyReportLinks.com Books
Great Books, Great Links, Great for Research!

The Report Links listed on the following four pages can save you hours of research time by **instantly** bringing you to the best Web sites relating to your report topic.

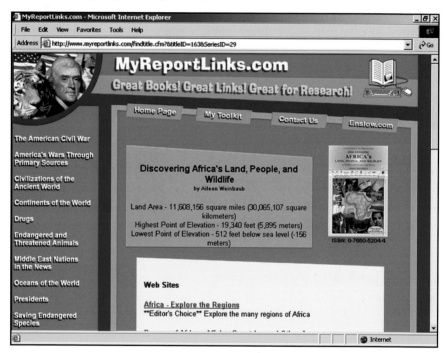

The pre-evaluated Web sites are your links to source documents, photographs, illustrations, and maps. They also provide links to dozens—even hundreds—of Web sites about your report subject.

MyReportLinks.com Books and the MyReportLinks.com Web site save you time and make report writing easier than ever!

Please see "To Our Readers" on the copyright page for important information about this book, the MyReportLinks.com Web site, and the Report Links that back up this book. Please enter **CAF7034** if asked for a password.

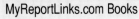

Report Links

 The Internet sites described below can be accessed at
http://www.myreportlinks.com

*EDITOR'S CHOICE

▶**Africa—Explore the Regions**
This site contains information on the many regions of Africa.
Learn about the way people in Africa live in their environment.

*EDITOR'S CHOICE

▶**Bureau of African Affairs: Country Information**
On this site from the Bureau of African Affairs, you can learn about
the different countries on the African continent.

*EDITOR'S CHOICE

▶**The Story of Africa**
This extensive Web site gives a detailed history of Africa, from the
beginnings of humankind to the present day.

*EDITOR'S CHOICE

▶**National Museum of African Art**
The National Museum of African Art Web site presents all types of art from all
areas of Africa. View the different exhibits that have appeared at the museum.

*EDITOR'S CHOICE

▶**AIDS: Africa in Peril**
This site from CNN provides in-depth information on the AIDS
epidemic in Africa. Learn about its effects, and the ongoing battle
against this terrible disease.

*EDITOR'S CHOICE

▶**Smithsonian Natural History Web: African Voices**
Created by the Smithsonian National Museum of Natural History, this site has a
detailed time line of African history from millions of years ago to the present day.

Report Links

**The Internet sites described below can be accessed at
http://www.myreportlinks.com**

▶ Africa

You can gather information from this Fact Monster site about the geography, climate, economy, and history of the African continent.

▶ Africa: Africana Online

Read about Africa on this site from Africana Online. Find information on regions, languages, religions, climate, animals, and more.

▶ Africa: Country-Specific Pages

The University of Pennsylvania's African Studies Center provides links to in-depth information about each African country.

▶ Africa Atlas

This site provides a map of all the countries in Africa. View a profile of each country, including current facts and historical information.

▶ Africa Focus: Sights and Sounds of a Continent

This site from the University of Wisconsin-Madison contains images of different aspects of African life. Listen to greetings, rites, songs, and drums by clicking on the audio files.

▶ allAfrica

This Web site provides news from all over Africa. Read about the current events that are happening in the different regions of the continent.

▶ Ancient Egypt

The British Museum presents information about Ancient Egypt. Topics include Egyptian life, mummification, pyramids, writing, and more.

▶ CultureFocus: African Safari photos

This site includes photos and information about various animals that people often see on an African safari.

Report Links

The Internet sites described below can be accessed at http://www.myreportlinks.com

▶**Desmond Tutu—Biography**

A brief biography of Desmond Tutu. He won the Nobel Peace Prize in 1984 for his work in the fight against apartheid in South Africa.

▶**DinoQuest Sahara**

On this site, you can follow a group of scientists as they search the African country of Niger for evidence of new dinosaur species.

▶**Ethnologue Country Index**

This site allows you to see which languages are spoken in each of the African nations. The site includes estimates of the number of people that speak each language.

▶**Fastest Snake**

Not only is the Black Mamba the fastest land snake in the world, it is also one of the most deadly snakes. Learn all about it here.

▶**GORP: Kilimanjaro National Park**

Mount Kilimanjaro is the highest mountain in Africa and one of the largest mountains in the world. Read about Kilimanjaro and the national park.

▶**Greatest Places: Namib Page**

On this site from the Science Museum of Minnesota, you can learn all about the Namib Desert and the plants and wildlife that inhabit this area.

▶**The Leakey Foundation—Louis S. B. Leakey**

Louis Leakey was born in Kenya and helped discover important hominid fossils in Africa. Read his biography on this site.

▶**Nelson Mandela**

On the *Time* magazine Web site, you can examine a biography of former South African President Nelson Mandela.

Report Links

The Internet sites described below can be accessed at http://www.myreportlinks.com

▶**Oakland Zoo—African Savannah**

The Oakland Zoo site provides information about, and photos of, some of the animals located in the African savannah.

▶**Pyramids—The Inside Story**

On this site from PBS, you can learn about the pyramids of Egypt. Be sure to take the virtual tour of the Great Pyramid.

▶**Robben Island Museum**

Learn about the history of Robben Island in South Africa. Primarily used as a prison for four hundred years, Robben Island held some famous inmates, including Nelson Mandela.

▶**Sahara**

This site from PBS gives an in-depth look into the Sahara Desert. Learn about the geography, people, and the wildlife of this vast desert.

▶**South African National Parks**

On this site, you can find information and the locations of the national parks located in South Africa.

▶**Stanley and Livingstone**

In 1869, British reporter and explorer Henry Morton Stanley went to Africa in search of explorer David Livingstone, who had not been heard from in several years. This site has a brief description of both men and what they discovered.

▶**Welcome to Tusk Trust Online!**

Tusk Trust is an organization dedicated to the conservation of African wildlife and habitat. Examine the different projects that they support.

▶**Wild Egypt—An Online Safari**

Take an online safari, and learn about the animals and habitat of the Egyptian region.

Africa Facts

Area*
11,608,156 square miles (30,065,107 square kilometers)[1]

Population
Estimated 840,000,000[2]

Five Most Populous Countries
- Nigeria (116,929,000)
- Egypt (69,080,000)
- Ethiopia (64,459,000)
- Democratic Republic of the Congo (52,522,000)
- South Africa (43,792,000)

Highest Point of Elevation
Mount Kilimanjaro, Tanzania 19,340 feet (5,895 meters)

Lowest Point of Elevation
Lake Àsal, Djibouti 512 feet below sea level (–156 meters)

Major Mountain Ranges
Ahaggar, Atlas, Drakensberg, Ruwenzori, Tibesti

Major Rivers
Congo, Limpopo, Niger, Nile, Orange, Zambezi

Major Religions
Traditional African religions and mythology, Islam, Christianity

Major Lakes
Albert, Chad, Nyasa, Tanganyika, Turkana, Victoria

Countries
Algeria, Angola, Benin, Botswana, Burkina Faso, Burundi, Cameroon, Cape Verde, Central African Republic, Chad, Comoros, Congo, Côte d'Ivoire (The Ivory Coast), Democratic Republic of the Congo, Djibouti, Egypt, Equatorial Guinea, Eritrea, Ethiopia, Gabon, Gambia, Ghana, Guinea, Guinea-Bissau, Kenya, Lesotho, Liberia, Libya, Madagascar, Malawi, Mali, Mauritania, Mauritius, Morocco, Mozambique, Namibia, Niger, Nigeria, Rwanda, São Tomé & Principe, Senegal, Seychelles, Sierra Leone, Somalia, South Africa, Sudan, Swaziland, Tanzania, Togo, Tunisia, Uganda, Zambia, Zimbabwe.

* All metric and Celsius measurements are approximate estimates.

Chapter 1

A Land of Contrasts

Africa is a land of contrasts. It is a place filled with hot, steamy jungles, dense forests, and sandy deserts. It is also a place of huge savannas and snowcapped peaks. Africa is home to the world's longest river and the world's biggest desert. It is a place filled with big cities and small communities. There are thousands of ethnic groups in Africa, and over a thousand languages are spoken there.

Africa is the second largest continent in the world. It has an area of 11,608,156 square miles (30,065,107 square kilometers).[1] All of the United States, Europe,

▲ *The Great Pyramids of Giza are located in Egypt. One of the seven ancient wonders of the world, they are very likely the most well-known landmark in Africa.*

India, and Japan can fit into the continent of Africa and there would still be room left over. The continent stretches about 5,000 miles (8,045 kilometers) from north to south. From east to west, at its widest point, the continent measures over 4,600 miles (7,401 kilometers). In all, fifty-three countries call Africa home.

▶ A Prehistoric Continent

Scientists have found African artifacts that date back to prehistoric times. Fossils of the first human beings have been found in Africa, telling us that mankind was born on this continent. Anthropologists—scientists who study fossils—have found bones of human ancestors dating back millions of years.

Louis Leakey was a famous archaeologist born in Kenya. He and his wife, Mary, excavated many sites during the mid-twentieth century. They discovered the *homo habilis* species, the first humanlike fossils ever found.

In 1974, a group of anthropologists found what they named the "Lucy" skeleton in the country of Tanzania. Lucy lived more than 3 million years ago. It is thought that she and others like her were the first humanlike creatures to make their own tools. Humanlike footprints dating back 3.6 million years have also been discovered in Tanzania.

Although Africa's history is longer than any other continent, it is only in recent decades that scientists have started to explore and understand it. This is partly because most people of Africa did not keep written records. Africans have used oral traditions to pass down important facts and stories. They kept their history alive by word of mouth, telling stories rather than writing them down. This is true for much of Africa, but not all of it.

▶ Ancient History

Besides being the birthplace of humankind, Africa was also home to many great ancient empires. One of these was the Egyptian Empire. The ancient Egyptians were very advanced. They built great temples and other structures that can still be seen five thousand years later. This includes the Great Pyramids of Giza, which is considered one of the wonders of the ancient world.

Ancient Egyptians recorded their history through hieroglyphs. These are pictures with certain meanings that tell a story. Many of these hieroglyphs can be seen on ancient buildings throughout Egypt. They tell scientists a lot about what life was like in ancient times.

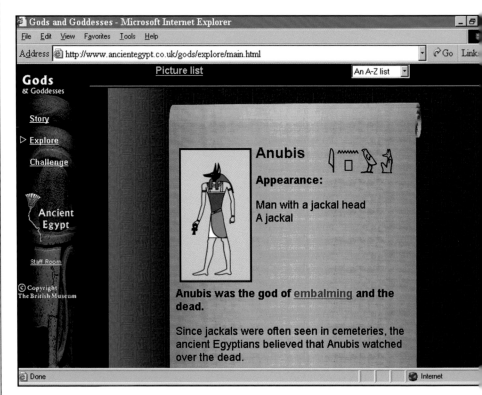

▲ *This drawing of Anubis is an example of a well-known Egyptian hieroglyph.*

▷ A Time of Change

For thousands of years, Africa was left unexplored by the rest of the world. In the last five hundred years, all of this has changed. Europeans, Arabs, and Turks came to Africa and exploited the continent. They purchased slaves from African nations and used them to work in other lands. The slaves were kept in brutal conditions and taken far away from their families. This practice permanently destroyed parts of Africa. Whole villages were burned. Families were torn apart. Millions of lives were sacrificed.

Even after slavery ended, Africa was still under foreign control. African countries were considered colonies of places such as Britain, France, Portugal, and Belgium. It was not until the mid-twentieth century that most African countries gained independence from their colonial rulers. Independence was a historical and long-awaited moment in African history. Unfortunately, many countries did not have the wealth or strength to survive without aid from other nations and international organizations.

Some of the nations in Africa are among the poorest in the world. Often these countries have poor soil for farming, and farmers cannot afford the equipment necessary to work the land. Also, the education system in much of Africa is not very strong. Africa has the lowest literacy rate in the world. Many people never learn to read. Corrupt governments have taken over some countries. These governments do not always do what is best for their people. Since independence, many wars have been fought in Africa. This is because different groups are fighting for control of their countries. In the meantime, the African people have suffered greatly. Many do not have running water. There is a lot of famine across the continent, and many are dying of starvation. Many Africans do not have

the basic means of survival that Western countries take for granted.

There is also much disease in Africa. The AIDS epidemic threatens to wipe out much of the population. With all of this, Africa still has the second highest population rate in the world.

▷ African Influence

Many different ways of life exist in Africa. In the country Botswana, some tribespeople hunt for food using a bow and arrow. In Tunisia, most people practice Islam. Muslim women cover their bodies from head to toe. In South

▲ *In some parts of Africa, people lack running water. In this image a woman is carrying a bucket of water on her head.*

Africa, the city of Johannesburg is a thriving, modern metropolis. The people there mainly dress the same as people living in European or North American cities.

Africa has influenced the rest of the world in many ways. African art is admired in museums around the world. African literature is also very popular in many countries. African foods are prepared and are often considered exotic delicacies to Westerners. African music has greatly influenced much of the music heard around the world today. This includes rhythm and blues, jazz, and gospel. Some of the finest craft work and beadwork can be found on this great continent.

Africa is a resource-rich continent, and people from many other countries come to trade with natives. Corporations will set up plants and offices in Africa to take advantage of the inexpensive labor. In this way, Europeans and Asians have also influenced the African way of life. For example, Europeans brought Christianity to Africa, and today many Africans practice that religion. Also, African countries have followed the lead of nations on other continents to set up farming and government policies.

Africa is a continent like no other. People from around the world come to explore Africa's wonders and to learn about the history that surrounds this continent.

Chapter 2

Land and Climate

The African continent can be divided in many ways. For the purpose of this book, it will be divided into five separate regions: Northern, Western, Eastern, Central, and Southern.

The countries of Northern Africa include Algeria, Morocco, Tunisia, Libya, Egypt, and the Sudan. In these countries, many people practice the Muslim religion and the majority of people are Arabic. The Sahara Desert separates these countries from the rest of Africa. All of the regions south of Northern Africa are called the sub-Sahara.

Western Africa includes the countries Mali, Burkina Faso, Niger, The Ivory Coast (Côte d'Ivoire), Guinea, Senegal, Mauritania, Benin, Togo, Cameroon, Guinea-Bissau, São Tomé and Principe, Cape Verde, Equatorial Guinea, Western Sahara, Liberia, Sierra Leone, Gambia, Ghana, and Nigeria. This is the first part of Africa that Europeans visited. For three centuries, much of the slave trade took place in these countries.

Eastern Africa includes Ethiopia, Eritrea, Somalia, Djibouti, Rwanda, Burundi, Uganda, Kenya, and Tanzania. There are hundreds of different communities in this region, each with their own language and customs. Ethiopia is the oldest independent state on the continent.

Central Africa includes the Democratic Republic of the Congo (formerly Zaire), the Congo, Gabon, Chad, Central African Republic, and the territories Zambia and Malawi. These areas are full of both wealth and poverty.

Southern Africa includes the countries of South Africa, Namibia, Lesotho, Swaziland, Botswana,

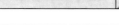
Zimbabwe, Mozambique, and Angola, as well as the islands of Madagascar, Mauritius, Seychelles, and Comoros. For a very long time, a white minority ruled these areas, even though most of the people that live there have dark skin.

The African Landscape

The physical features of Africa can be broken up into three major regions. They are the Northern Plateau, Central and Southern Plateau, and Eastern Highlands.

▲ A map of the African continent.

The natural features of Africa have played an important role in the continent's history. Europeans who settled in Africa chose to live at higher elevations, such as in Kenya, Ethiopia, and South Africa. This is because temperatures in higher regions are often cooler, and insects, such as mosquitoes, are less common.

The Northern Plateau

The Sahara Desert makes up much of the Northern Plateau. Mountains can be found along the edges of this region. The Atlas Mountains are in the northwest. They are a chain of mountains that run from Morocco to Tunisia. The Cameroon Mountain Range is in the southern part of this region. Lake Chad is another feature of the Northern Plateau. It can be found almost in the center of the plateau.

The Sahara Desert

The Sahara was not always the vast desert it is today. Millions of years ago, it was a fertile region. Many plants and trees grew there, and animals roamed freely. There was even an abundance of water in this region. Over a period of time, the land went through many changes. Mountains crumbled, and large rocks turned into tiny grains of sand. The air began to grow dry. Rivers disappeared. Today, the Sahara covers over 3.5 million square miles (9,064,960 square kilometers), stretching from the Atlantic Ocean to the Red Sea.

Many people who live in the Sahara are nomads. They live in tents and travel from place to place seeking food and water. They travel along ancient routes, using stars to guide them. Others live on oases in the desert. An oasis is a small community, usually near a water source, where

Tools Search Notes Discuss

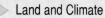

Africa Focus Record Display - Microsoft Internet Explorer

Edit View Favorites Tools Help

dress http://webcat.library.wisc.edu:3092/WebZ/FETCH?sessionid=01-37619-552874269&recno=2& Go Links

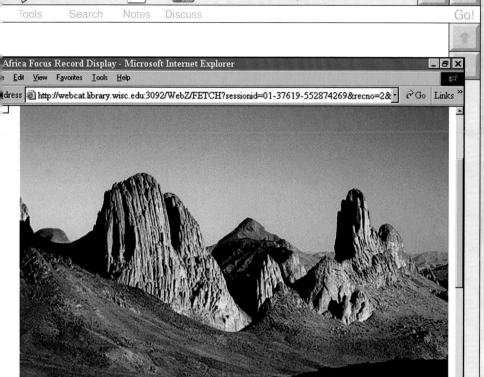

Internet

▲ *The Sahara is the world's largest desert. Once, the land that is now the Sahara was a fertile region.*

people can live and raise crops. Temperature highs have been known to reach 130°F (54°C) in the Sahara.

The Central and Southern Plateau

The Central and Southern Plateau of Africa is much higher than the Northern Plateau. It includes both the west central and southern parts of Africa. The Congo River in the western central region, and the Kalahari Desert in the southern region, are two important features in this part of Africa. The Drakensberg Mountains stretch for about 700 miles (1,126 kilometers) along the southeastern coast of Africa. The High Veld Plateau is located in the extreme south.

The Eastern Highlands

This region is the highest part of Africa and is located on the eastern coast of the continent. These highlands stretch from the Red Sea to the Zambezi River. Average elevation along the coast is 5,000 feet (1,524 meters) above sea level. Parts of the coast rise to as high as 10,000 feet (3,048 meters) above sea level. There many well-known volcanic peaks in this area, including Mount Kilimanjaro, Mount Kenya, and Mount Elgon.

The Great Rift Valley

The Great Rift Valley is located within the Eastern Highlands. This is a huge crack in the earth that stretches almost 4,000 miles (6,436 kilometers) across the continent. This valley is as deep as 2,000 feet (610 meters) in some places. There are parts that are over 100 miles (160 kilometers) wide. The Great Rift Valley was formed by volcanic eruptions, as well as the movement of the earth's tectonic plates. Bill Bryson, a famous travel writer, visited the Great Rift Valley. He was amazed by what he saw. "As you head south and west of Nairobi there comes a place where the ground just falls away and there spread out below you is the biggest open space you have ever seen: The Great Rift Valley."[1]

The volcanoes along the Rift Valley provide fertile soil for growing crops. This has allowed many people to settle in this region. There are also lakes around the Rift Valley that provide an abundance of fish.

Major Bodies of Water

Although there are many dry regions in Africa, it is also a continent surrounded by water. The major waterways

The Great Rift Valley is a huge crack in the earth's surface. The volcanoes along the Great Rift Valley have created soil that is good for growing crops. The valley's eastern branch runs through the central parts of Ethiopia, Tanzania, and Kenya.

include the Mediterranean Sea, Red Sea, Gulf of Aden, Indian Ocean, and Atlantic Ocean.

The major lakes are Victoria, Nyasa, Tanganyika, Chad, and Volta. Lake Victoria is the largest lake in Africa and the second largest freshwater lake in the world.

There are six huge rivers in Africa. They are the Nile (in Eastern Africa), Congo (Central Africa), Niger (Northwestern Africa), Zambezi (Southeastern Africa), Orange (Southern Africa), Senegal (Northwestern Africa), and Limpopo (Southeastern Africa). Most of these rivers have spots that are too dangerous to pass through. This is partly because of underwater sandbars and great rapids.

The Nile

The Nile River is the longest river in the world. It has been a source of survival for the African people for thousands of

years. Egypt, often called "the Gift of the Nile," could not have grown into a great empire if not for this river. The river starts out as two branches: the White Nile and the Blue Nile. The White Nile begins its journey in Uganda. The Blue Nile starts in Ethiopia. They meet in Khartoum, the capital of Sudan. The river and its tributaries run through nine countries and flow a total of 4,160 miles (6,693 kilometers). Even today, the Nile provides food, fertile land, and a mode of transportation. Farmers who live along the Nile wait for the summer floods. These floods leave rich soil behind for growing crops.

▶ **The Congo**

The Congo River is the second longest river in Africa. It stretches 2,718 miles (4,373 kilometers), beginning its journey near the borders of Zambia and the Democratic

▲ *The Uganda Murchison Falls on the Nile River.*

Republic of Congo. This is an ever-changing river. Some parts of the river are very wide while others are incredibly narrow. Some parts are also very deep while others are so shallow a person could easily stand in the middle of it. There are also many waterfalls along this river. The famous ones are Livingston Falls, Inga Falls, and Stanley Falls.

▶ The African Climate

There are several different climate zones throughout the continent. The central part of the continent and the eastern coast of Madagascar have tropical rain forests. The average temperature in this region of Africa is about 80°F (26.7°C).

The northern and southern parts of Africa are known for tropical savanna climates. In this region, the summers are wet and the winters are dry. However, extreme northern and southern parts of Africa have what is known as the steppe climate. The steppe climate is much drier than the savanna climate.

Africa also has many arid, or desert, climate zones. These include the Sahara, Kalahari, and Namib deserts. The "Horn" of Africa is its most eastern part. It includes the countries of Eritrea, Ethiopia, Djibouti, and Somalia. The Horn of Africa has an arid climate as well. Arid climates in Africa are so hot, they often receive less than 10 inches (25.4 centimeters) of rainfall a year. This means that water supply in these regions is limited. People here must store water to survive the year.

The Mediterranean climate zones are found in the extreme northwest and the extreme southwest regions of Africa. These climate zones have wet, but mild winters and dry summers.

Plant and Animal Life

Africa is home to some of the most interesting wildlife on the planet. All over Africa there are many natural environments in which animals can roam free. National parks protect animals in Kenya, Tanzania, Zimbabwe, and South Africa. Baboons can be found in the mountains of Ethiopia. The savannas in the east and south are filled with lions, cheetahs, giraffes, elephants, and antelope. Rwanda

▲ Many giraffes can be found in the savannas of Eastern Africa.

and Uganda are known for their wild mountain gorillas. The Sudan is home to white rhinoceroses. Crocodiles and hippopotamuses live in and around bodies of water throughout the continent. The African elephant, gorillas, and the white rhinoceros are all endangered species.

There are two zones for animal life in Africa. They are the North and Northwestern Zone and the Ethiopian Zone.

The North and Northwestern Zone

As the name suggests, this zone includes all of North and Northwest Africa, including the Sahara Desert. Animals found in this zone are sheep, goats, horses, camels, African red deer, and ibex. In the Sahara, desert foxes, hares, gazelles, and a small leaping rodent called a jerboa can all be found roaming freely.

The Ethiopian Zone

This zone includes all of sub-Saharan Africa, meaning anything below the Sahara Desert. Zebras, giraffes, buffalo, African elephants, rhinoceroses, baboons, and a variety of monkeys are found here, along with lions, leopards, cheetahs, hyenas, jackals, and mongooses. The largest ape in the world, the gorilla, can be found in the hot rain forests of Africa. Monkeys, flying squirrels, bats, and lemurs also thrive in this region. People from all over the world come to see African wildlife. Author E. Jefferson Murphy wrote, "At Kenya National Park, it is possible to drive slowly along the road in a taxi and see wild elephants. . . . [And] Murchison Falls National Park in Uganda has the largest concentration of elephants in the world."[1]

Birds, Insects, and Reptiles

In Africa, there are many different kinds of birds, reptiles, fish, and insects. Some birds found on this continent

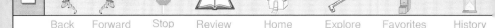
include guinea fowl, pelicans, goliath herons, flamingoes, storks, egrets, ibis, and ostrich. There are also over two thousand species of fish in Africa.

There are many types of insects in Africa. Some cause great damage and spread disease. Mosquitoes in Africa often carry malaria. Other problem-causing insects are driver ants, termites, locusts, and tsetse flies.

Africa is also a land known for its reptiles, including lizards, crocodiles, and tortoises. Poisonous snakes can be found living throughout Africa, including the mamba. Constricting snakes kill their prey by squeezing them to death. The python, found in Western Africa, and boa constrictors, found in Madagascar, are two types of con-stricting snakes found in Africa.

▶ Plant Life

The vegetation in Africa depends on the climate zone. The less rainfall there is in an area, the less vegetation. In hot, steamy, rain forests, there are thick shrubs, mosses, tall evergreens, oil palms, and many other tropical hardwood trees. Mountain forest zones are filled with shrubs, oil palms, hard-wood trees, and conifers. The savanna woodland zone is covered with grass

Ostrich are a unique type of bird found in Africa. Their long necks allow them to hunt for food deep in the soil.

and shrubs, along with many different types of trees. The savanna grasslands are known for low grasses, shrubs, and small deciduous trees. The thornbush zone has thin grass and a scattering of trees. The sub-desert scrub zone has grass and scattered low shrubs. The desert zone of Africa has the least amount of rainfall of all the zones. This area has little or no vegetation.

▶ Growing Food

Much of the soil in Africa is poor. This is due to heavy rainfall and high temperatures. The soil does not have enough vitamins and minerals to grow crops. A lot of communities in Africa do not have modern equipment to make planting easier.

In recent years, people from humanitarian organizations have traveled to Africa to help teach new ways to work the land. An organization called CARE is one of many that help fight poverty in Africa. CARE teaches farmers how to best use their land. The idea is that the farmers will then teach their neighbors what they have learned. In this way, many people can benefit from the work CARE does. During travel writer Bill Bryson's trip to Africa, he met a farmer named Gumbo. CARE had helped Gumbo raise a model farm. "Until 1999, Gumbo scratched a living raising maize and millet and a few chickens. . . . [Today] He grows peas, tomatoes, bananas, pineapples, passion fruit, mangos, and much else. Only sweet potatoes have been a failure: some livestock broke through a fence and gobbled them up."[2]

People of Africa also grow crops that are native to other lands. People from Asia introduced rice, yams, and bananas to Africa. Americans have brought over corn and sweet potatoes. These crops can grow in many areas of

▲ *These woman are preparing lunch at a farming co-op near Masvingo, Zimbabwe. In rural areas, communities of people often decide to purchase land together.*

Africa. This had made it easier for people to settle in certain places throughout the continent.

▶ A Way of Life

In Africa, people eat what they grow. Often, farming communities are small. Many do not trade or sell their food. They do not get new things from other communities. They must depend on their own community to survive.

The ownership of land is thought about very differently in Africa than it is in Western countries. African communities do not buy land to live on. In rural areas, if a community decides together to clear land to grow food, that land becomes a part of the community.

People and Culture

African tradition is very important to the different communities throughout the continent. Each group has its own special customs and religious rituals. In many communities, food, religion, dress, and daily life have remained the same for hundreds of years.

▶ Family Life

Strong family ties are very important in African culture. Families are often very large. Cousins, aunts, uncles, sisters, and brothers all remain very close to one another. In some communities, men may marry two or more women

▲ These students listen intently at a school in Ouelessebougou, Mali.

at a time. When a woman gets married, she will join her husband's family. If the husband dies, she will still stay with his family and may marry one of her husband's brothers. Many times, wives and children have their own hut.

Tradition

Children are taught all the traditions of their community from an early age. Everyone in the group takes part in raising the children. As they grow, they are given more responsibility and are shown how to help grow food for their community. They are also taught the rites and customs of their community.

Language

There are over one thousand different languages in Africa. That is more languages than are spoken on any other continent. One of the major languages in Africa is Swahili. Over 50 million people speak this language in East and Central Africa. Other major languages include Fulfulde, Hausa, and Yoruba. In North Africa, the major language is Arabic.

European influence has played a part in African language. Many African people speak English, French, or Portuguese as well as a tribal language or Arabic.

Dialects

There are many different dialects within Africa. Dialects form when people who speak the same language move apart. After hundreds of years, the language starts to slightly change.

In Africa, the way something is said is as important as what is being said. One word may have many different meanings. The tone or how a word is being used is the

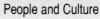
only way a person can know for sure what is meant. In the Bambara language, the word "ba" means "river" when said in a high-pitched voice. The same word said in a low voice means "goat."

▶ Oral Tradition

People in Africa rely on oral tradition to pass down their history from generation to generation. People learn about their ancestors, rituals, and customs by listening to stories. They also learn about farming techniques and animal herding in this way. Stories, riddles, and poems are also a very important part of African tradition.

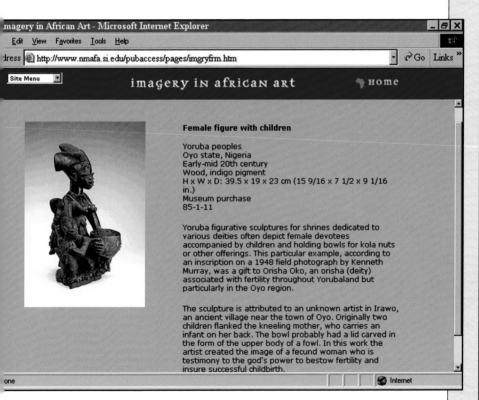

imagery in African Art - Microsoft Internet Explorer

Edit　View　Favorites　Tools　Help

dress ⊞ http://www.nmafa.si.edu/pubaccess/pages/imgryfrm.htm ▾ ∂ Go | Links »

Site Menu ▾

imagery in african art 🌍 HOME

Female figure with children

Yoruba peoples
Oyo state, Nigeria
Early-mid 20th century
Wood, indigo pigment
H x W x D: 39.5 x 19 x 23 cm (15 9/16 x 7 1/2 x 9 1/16 in.)
Museum purchase
85-1-11

Yoruba figurative sculptures for shrines dedicated to various deities often depict female devotees accompanied by children and holding bowls for kola nuts or other offerings. This particular example, according to an inscription on a 1948 field photograph by Kenneth Murray, was a gift to Orisha Oko, an orisha (deity) associated with fertility throughout Yorubaland but particularly in the Oyo region.

The sculpture is attributed to an unknown artist in Irawo, an ancient village near the town of Oyo. Originally two children flanked the kneeling mother, who carries an infant on her back. The bowl probably had a lid carved in the form of the upper body of a fowl. In this work the artist created the image of a fecund woman who is testimony to the god's power to bestow fertility and insure successful childbirth.

one ● Internet

▲ African statues and other works of art are sold or displayed throughout the world. The wood figurine shown here was created in Nigeria by a member of the Yoruba people.

Religion

There are many different religions in Africa. In the North and part of the West most people practice Islam. Many Africans also believe in the Christian religion. European missionaries brought Christianity to Africa during colonial times. Many wars have been fought over religious beliefs.

Traditional African religions are also practiced all over the continent. These religions are often referred to as African mythology. Many believe in the magic of certain people or objects. They also believe in different types of spirits. Many African cultures believe in serving gods and goddesses through rituals. They also show their dedication to their religion through the arts.

Arts

Some of the earliest art in the world comes from Africa. Rock art has been found in the caves of Namibia dating back to 25,500 B.C. These include images of animals painted on rock. Unfortunately, most African art has not survived. This is because much of it was made from materials that could not stand the test of time, including wood, plant fibers, and cloth.

In Egypt, one can still see many statues, sculptures, and even decorative tombs from ancient times. However, much of the rest of African art is from the 1800s or later. Most African art is made for a specific purpose. This is very different than Western art, which is usually meant to be admired. Art in Africa is often used in religious or social settings and is very symbolic. For example, wooden or clay figures may be used to try to contact spirits. However, art in Africa may also be used to fulfill everyday household needs. This may include baskets, water vessels, and eating utensils. Each culture has its own way of creating art. Beadwork, metalwork, and fabrics, such as the kente cloth, a colorful cloth with many patterns, are all part of African art.

Masks

Some Africans wear masks during celebrations and ceremonies. It is thought that the mask will protect the person who wears it. Most masks are made of wood, but some are made of cloth. They are also decorated with beads and painted. They can be worn to ward off danger, celebrate a certain season, or to honor an important visitor. In most African cultures, only men wear masks.

Body Art

Many groups in Africa believe in decorating their bodies. They may wear certain jewelry, or they may scar their skin. Both represent status within a community. Besides

▲ Masks are an important part of many African religious celebrations and rituals. This craftsman stands with two masks that he created.

looking nice, jewelry may be used in ceremonies or to ward off evil spirits.

Furniture

Stools and headrests are African art. Stools are usually carved out of wood and are decorated with detailed patterns. Some stools are used for the home, while others are used in ceremonies. The Ashanti people believe that when a person sits down on a stool, his or her spirit becomes part of the stool.

Headrests are often used instead of pillows. These look a lot like small stools with a curved platform for the head. The bottom part of the headrest is usually very decorative. Headrests serve to keep hairstyles in place during sleep. The Shona people believe that certain headrests allow people to communicate with the spirits of their ancestors.

Sports

Soccer is the most popular sport in Africa. Outside the United States, soccer is called football. Europeans introduced soccer to African people. Since then, local teams from Morocco, Nigeria, Cameroon, and South Africa have contributed greatly to the sport.

Cricket is another well-liked sport in Africa, also introduced by the Europeans. Long-distance running has become popular, too. Kip Keino from Kenya and Haile Gebreselassie from Ethiopia have become well known throughout the world for their great running ability.

Economy

Africa is rich in natural resources and has a growing tourism industry. Even so, it is a very poor continent. Until the nineteenth century, Europeans traded with Africans along the west coast. Until this time, most people did not realize the riches that could be found inside the continent. In 1867, and then again in 1884, diamonds and gold were discovered in South Africa. People from all over the world started pouring into the continent to seek their fortunes. This changed the course of African history.

▲ Mt. Kilimanjaro, located in Tanzania, is a popular spot for mountain climbers. The natural beauty of Mt. Kilimanjaro also makes it a very popular landmark.

Natural Resources

After gold and diamonds were discovered, it was realized that Africa had an abundance of other resources as well. There are more types of minerals on this continent than in any other part of the world. Fossil fuels, including coal, petroleum, and natural gas, are plentiful. Oil is an important resource in Western Africa. Iron and coal are found throughout many parts of the continent. Large amounts of copper can be found in the Democratic Republic of Congo and Zambia. Other resources found in Africa include bauxite, manganese, nickel, lithium, titanium, and phosphates, along with clays, mica, sulfur, salt, natron, graphite, limestone, and gypsum. Africa depends on trading these resources with other countries to survive. It is thought that there are still many places in Africa that have an abundance of resources yet to be discovered.

Agriculture

Agricultural goods plentiful in Africa include cotton, tea, coffee, cocoa, rubber, cloves, and tobacco. Unfortunately, most Africans have not benefited from these resources. Europeans have controlled much of these industries.

Water Shortages

One thing Africa is short on is water. Ethiopia, Mauritania, Senegal, Mali, Burkina Faso, Niger, and Chad have all suffered from long droughts. This has made it very hard to grow food. People have starved, animals have died, and farmland has been ruined because of a lack of water.

Clean water is very important for survival. In villages that have clean water, there is much less risk of disease. If one does get sick, though, he or she may not be able to get the proper care. Basic health care is not available in much of Africa. The average person only lives to the age of fifty-five. That is much lower than on other continents.

Many governments and humanitarian organizations are trying to come up with ways to help their people. Countries are working to establish trade with other continents. This will bring money into Africa. Groups such as the Organization for African Unity also work to help create economic and social development throughout Africa.

▲ *The camel is a popular form of transportation in the African desert. This is because camels can go for long periods before needing water.*

▷ Transportation

Under favorable conditions, it would be possible to drive the length of Africa. Unfortunately many factors have made travel hard in parts of Africa. In Egypt, travel is easy. In the northern part of Sudan and Ethiopia, travel becomes much more difficult. This is because there is a lot of fighting in these countries. Swamps, a lack of bridges, and years of fighting make it next to impossible to travel through southern Sudan.

Unlike other continents, there is not a lot of modern technology in Africa. In parts of Africa, there are few

▲ Each year thousands of tourists flock to African countries to go on safaris or view the continent's wildlife in national parks. This elephant roams the land in the nation of South Africa.

paved roads and even fewer railroads. Many roads that have been built are in great need of repair.

Tourism

Africa is a place like no other. Many people from all over the world come to Africa in search of adventure, and they are seldom disappointed. The Atlas Mountains of Morocco is a hot spot for vacationers, and the city of Fes, Morocco, is for people looking for new sights, sounds, and tastes. Namibia has beautiful landscapes. Estosha National Park is the place for bird-watchers. Sinai is a scuba divers' paradise where many come to explore the coral reefs of the Red Sea. South Africa has thriving cities with incredible parks. Tanzania has more game animals than any other place on Earth, and safari is a big industry. People from all over the world come to Tanzania to climb Kilimanjaro, the highest mountain in Africa. Zimbabwe is great for white-water rafting, and Egypt is the place to study ancient history. These are just a few of the many things that the continent of Africa has to offer.

Chapter 6

Exploration and History

Africa was called "the Dark Continent" by Europeans. This is because it was unknown to Europeans for a long time. Also, many Europeans mistakenly believed that the continent lacked civilized cultures. In truth, Africa had been trading with Asia to the east as far back as the first century A.D. Some products from Africa eventually made their way to Europe from Asia, but no one ever questioned from where those products really came. Yet, Ancient Rome had treaties with Ancient Carthage as early as 508 B.C. Carthage was built in present-day Tunisia.

▲ During the 1500s, Timbuktu is said to have been the richest city in all of Africa. This drawing is an artist's idea of what Timbuktu might have looked like.

▷ African Kingdoms

In ancient times, Africa had many thriving kingdoms. Ancient Egypt is one of the oldest and most studied kingdoms. Meroe was the capital of Ethiopia in 450 B.C. Kilwa was a port city on the east coast of Africa during the fourteenth century. Timbuktu is located in the country of Mali. During the sixteenth century, Timbuktu was the richest city in all of Africa. Leo Africanus, a Spanish Moor said, "Here in Timbuktu there are great stores of doctors, judges, priests, and other learned men."[1]

▷ Colonization and Slave Trade

After the Europeans discovered Africa's riches, they began setting up colonies. They seized control from tribal dictatorships and exploited the land. Africans had to live under European rule. Many Africans now had to follow the laws imposed on them by the Europeans.

Slavery had occurred in Africa since ancient times. However, from the 1400s through the 1800s, millions of Africans were sold into slavery to merchants from European nations. With European colonization of the Western Hemisphere, the practice grew to numbers larger than any other time in history.

European countries that owned colonies in the Americas started using slaves from Africa to work the land. Slave ships carried people from West Africa and brought them over to the Americas. The slaves were often treated brutally aboard these ships. They lived in horrible conditions and were often beaten. People in Africa trying to find slaves to sell burnt entire villages to make the people that lived there run out into the open so they could be caught and sold. Slaves were then chained and shackled around the neck. Many did not even survive the trip

▲ European countries carved up the continent of Africa into many separate colonies. This illustration shows where these European countries had their possessions.

across the ocean. West African traders often exchanged slaves for guns, cloth, and ceramics.

Once in the Americas, slaves had to oftentimes work twelve-hour days in the field. Many of them worked on plantations in what became the southern United States. They also worked in mines, forests, and on ranches in such places as the West Indies and throughout the Caribbean Islands. Slavery forced Africans from their homes, broke up families, and destroyed whole communities.

Independence

By the 1960s, many African nations won, or were granted their independence from European rule. Yet, many countries no longer had the resources to govern themselves. Africa was faced with the task of bringing together old traditions and new ways of living. Botswana has used ideas from both the British government and African tradition. Free press is allowed, and their political system continues to grow. Kenya is working toward similar goals. It is the center of political and economic life in East Africa. Senegal is also promoting these ideas. Many nations have looked back to the days of their old kingdoms. Many countries have been renamed. For example, the former Gold Coast is once again called Ghana.

The idea of democracy is very new to African nations. Many countries now allow free elections. Unfortunately, this does not always promise a stable government. There are a lot of uprisings in Africa. Military rule is still in place in some areas. Both military and other groups have overthrown governments by force throughout the continent. One such place where peace has been difficult to achieve is the Congo. Cultural differences, dictatorship, and former foreign rule have made it very hard to find solutions.

Apartheid

The country of South Africa is different from the rest of the countries on the continent. This is because many Europeans live in South Africa. In 1948, laws were made to separate blacks, Asians, and people of mixed descent from white people. This practice of segregation was known as apartheid. Black people had to have a special pass if they wanted to go into white areas. At one time, about 87 percent of South Africa was for white people

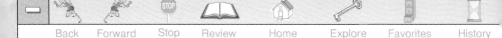

▲ *In addition to the rural areas, Africa also has many modern cities. Nairobi, Kenya, (shown here) is considered the center of economy for Eastern Africa.*

only, even though there were more blacks in South Africa than white people. This led to a lot of violence in South Africa as black citizens spoke out.

Nelson Mandela was one of the most important leaders against apartheid. His beliefs landed him in prison where he was tried for treason. Mandela refused to change his political views in exchange for freedom. He was released from prison in 1990 and continued to practice his beliefs. Mandela was elected president of South Africa after apartheid ended. He won a Nobel Peace Prize for his work in 1993.

Archbishop Desmond Tutu was another important leader during the time of apartheid. He fought for justice and equality and was considered a symbol of peace. He said, "My vision is of . . . a free South Africa, where all of us, black and white, together will walk; where all of us, black and white together, will hold hands. . . . "[2]

The practice of apartheid ended in 1991, and black South Africans were finally given the right to vote in their own government in 1994. In a similar situation, the country of Namibia won independence from a white minority government in 1991.

▷ AIDS Epidemic

Disease is a big problem in Africa. The AIDS epidemic has hit Africa very hard. It is thought that AIDS first started in Central Africa. Many of the poor countries in that area and in Southern Africa do not have good health-care systems. They also lack the education needed to stop the spread of AIDS. Humanitarian organizations are doing what they can to help educate people about the disease and spread awareness. Lack of funds, poor transportation, and limited resources make this very difficult.

▷ Africa Today

Almost every nation in Africa has gained independence. Since the 1960s, over twenty wars have been fought. People still fight for control of the government, and poverty among the people is still a big concern. At the end of the twentieth century many Africans were still struggling for democracy.

Even though Africa faces great challenges, it is a land of possibilities. Slowly, new technology is coming to Africa. People are able to do things and live in places they never dreamed of. Humanitarian organizations and foreign aid, along with a commitment from African governments, will hopefully lead Africa toward a bright future.

Africa Facts

1. Figures for land areas were taken from *Time Almanac 2003*, Borgna Bruner, editor.

2. Population estimates from Population Division, Department of Economic and Social Affairs, United Nations Secretariat—The 2001 Revision. Reprinted by One World Nations Online, "Countries of Africa," *Nationsonline .org*, n.d., <www.nationsonline.org/oneworld/africa.htm> (January 5, 2004).

Chapter 1. A Land of Contrasts

1. Borgna Bruner, ed., *Time Almanac 2003* (Boston: Information Please, 2002), p. 487.

Chapter 2. Land and Climate

1. Bill Bryson, *Bill Bryson's African Diary* (New York: Broadway Books, 2002), p. 18.

Chapter 3. Animal and Plant Life

1. E. Jefferson Murphy, *Understanding Africa* (New York: Thomas Y. Crowell, 1978), p. 26.

2. Bill Bryson, *Bill Bryson's African Diary* (New York: Broadway Books, 2002), p. 46.

Chapter 6. Exploration and History

1. Leo Africanus, as quoted in *Land and Peoples: Africa Volume 1* (Danbury, Conn.: Grolier, 1997), p. 30.

2. Michelle Landis, "Desmond Tutu," *Waging Peace*, 2002, <http://www.wagingpeace.org/articles/peaceheroes/ desmond_tutu.html> (September 26, 2003).

Further Reading

Canesso, Claudia. *South Africa*. New York: Chelsea House, 1998.

Diagram Group Staff. *Peoples of West Africa*. New York: Facts on File, 1997.

Hart, George. *Eyewitness Ancient Egypt*. New York: Dorling Kindersley, 2000.

Jenson-Elliot, Cynthia L. *East Africa*. Farmington Hills, Mich.: Gale Group, 2002.

Knight, Margy Burns, et. al. *Africa Is Not a Country*. Brookfield, Conn.: Millbrook Press, 2002.

Knight, Tim. *Journey into Africa: A Nature Discovery Trip*. New York: Oxford University Press, 2002.

Martell, Hazel Mary. *Exploring Africa*. Columbus, Ohio.: McGraw-Hill Children's Publishing, 1997.

Peterson, David. *Africa*. New York: Scholastic Library Publishing, 1998.

Thomas, Velma Maia. *Lest We Forget: The Passage from Africa to Slavery and Emancipation*. New York: Random House Value Publishing, 1997.

Worth, Richard. *Stanley and Livingstone and the Exploration of Africa in World History*. Berkeley Heights, N.J.: Enslow Publishers, Inc., 2000.

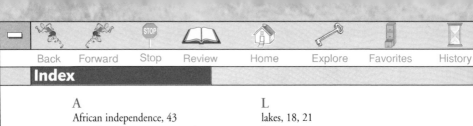